言葉 宝物 は

Words are treasure....

Threkjshanelle

TreasureHouse

TreasureHouse

◆

The Best of Threkjshanelle

Jonathan Christopher Martin

RellianStorm Publishing

Colorado Springs

TreasureHouse

The Best of Threkjshanelle

All Rights Reserved © 2011 by Jonathan Christopher Martin

RellianStorm Publishing

ISBN: 978-0-9815880-0-1

For information, address:

RellianStorm

722 E. Las Animas

Colorado Springs, Colorado

80903

Printed in the United States of America

Acknowledgements

Photo credits: Jonathan Christopher Martin
                   Stacey Kaylor
                   Andy Cooper

Model credits: Natasha Martin
                   Kaitlynn Priest-Martin
                   Linda Fera
                   Joseph Masters
                   Jamaica Lee Aderholt
                   Bunny Bee Bracke

Proto-copying: Jim Heaton
Graphic design: Julia Mastley
                   Paul Carhart
                   Maximillian Emert

Linguist: (Japanese)   Jessie Tomich

Linguist: (Italian)   Toni Cody

Technical consultant: Jamie Kelley
                        Marla Koupal

"Half a Mind to Halve a Mind II" courtesy of Andy Cooper

Special thanks to: Kendall John

Beginnings ~ Endings

In the year 2000, Jonathan Martin embarked upon a journey of written self-expression. The result was Threkjshanelle. The word itself, meaning collection or gathering was borrowed from the Martin short story, *Relliad*.

As a young teen, Jonathan admired Ron Glass' portrayal of the suave detective Ron Harris, on the hit 80's television show *Barney Miller*. Towards the end of the show's run, the Harris character began to pursue a career in writing. Eventually, this inspired Jonathan to write his own ticket to worlds and words yet unknown....

Dreaming Out Loud

The Best of Threkjshanelle: Collection One

I Wayward

Thunder rode the dusty plain
As it roared it called my name
Where's my love to stand by me
To take my soul and set me free
Rescue me…
Come my way…
Fatal kiss, melt my heart, stone
Break away…
Let me be…
Rebel breed, I'm on my own

Walking the Shadowlands

Scan the wreckage of my mind
Can you see all the pain?
Scan the wreckage of my soul
It is such an awful strain
Memories I'd left behind
Suddenly, find they are haunting me
There's no meaning to my life
I am a void unto myself
Heart of stone, and blood of ice
Tenderness is on a shelf
Longing for a joy unknown
To my bleak and wretched past
Memories I'd left behind
Suddenly, find they are killing me
No new horizon (They are killing me)
Is there no future (They are killing me.)

Thug Boy

I do murder, I do plunder,
Do you like me?
I don't care...

Is it even any wonder
Why I'm rampant everywhere

Running through the fields of normal
Searching for my sanity

Threatened only by my future
God! What has become of me?

Sealing my fate, no redemption
On my way to hell I go

Strap me to the chair of rapture
Sizzle as the juices flow

All is light; turning to darkness
Covered by the earth you see,

I did murder, I did plunder
Lord I pray, mercy on me

Please.

Tejshaana

All the Nova battles rage
As I turn, every page of my life
I realize I can't survive
All of the destruction
Going on around me
How can I function?
It really does astound me,
Sometimes.

On the edge of hoping now
As I turn, every page of my life
I realize to my surprise
Victory is coming
Ships on the horizon
Galaxy freedom!
Feel like I'm electric,
I'm free.

Victory is coming
Ships on the horizon
Galaxy freedom!
Feel like I'm electric…. I'm free!!

Revenge is Coming

Revenge is coming my beloved…
Like the chill of winter winds,
Like the rain when storms begin,
Like twisted metal in a heart.

Revenge is coming my most hated…
To see you bleed,
To hear you cry,
To feel you ache, then watch you die.

Bliss is coming, no mistake…
When souls are burning in my wake,
When threats are all but swept aside,
When is dead your selfish pride.

Spider

Distant storms, they echo
Your mouth, it tastes like rain
A quenching of desire
As I am yours again
Come into my garden
Or could it be a web?
Where your love is captured
Forever…

Always…

I remember a time of rain
You never left my side,
I see
Sometimes you even carried me
From one day to another
I recall my heart was slain
You took me in your arms and said
I resurrect you from the dead
And swear to love no other…

Multi-Breed

To be alone in a crowd
Living life as a shadow
Of hatred spoken out loud
What does it matter though
To change a world,
You must destroy it
And start again

To change a mind
You must annoy it
Reshape and make it bend

Multi-breed, misunderstood
Multi-breed, you wish 'they' would
Fade into their darkness…

Stacey Kaylor © 2010

Chasing Starlight & Fireflies

The Best of Threkjshanelle: Collection Two

Sharon

An Irish wind
My life be blessed

A sacred bond beyond a kiss

Time is fleeting
Though love stands still

At times you wonder if you are missed

No, I have not forgotten…

Como Veranos en Jamaica

The rain is falling once again
On sands drenched in my longing
Flowing winds carry desire

Her desire
Her in intent

To render me

Ever wanting
Ever spent

My gaze is falling once again
On a beauty
That leaves me haunted

Someone's lover
Someone's treasure

Someone's heart
Beyond all measure

Her very presence
Makes time stand still…

Tequila

My true and only friend
When no one loves me
When no one cares

You sooth tense bindings
Set free my arrogance

I need no other for the night
My blended lover, intoxicator

Embrace me tightly
So I may fly

Little Whisper

I am sleeping, not for long

Little whisper, my wee love
Only if you knew how to
View the ways I cherish you through
Eyes of mine, eyes of joy, eyes of pride

You woke me with your little wantings
One water-filled glass,
Untold stories of trolls under bridges

Kittens for Christmas
And cheese toast at breakfast
To say I love you is not enough, or say
You are mine, not bold enough
Just because the world must see and hold you
As I do, my little whisper

Booshka Bear

In echoes of myself

Little remembrances
Of younger days
Very soon you'll grow up and fly away
Ever always my Booshka Bear

Years fly by, yet your heart remains
Overflowing with a light that is
Unique and regal

Now and then I smile
As I think of all you wish to be
There is a love that flows from you
And makes my rainy days
Shy away
Have a life of sweet tomorrows and know that I
Always love you

Letter on an Autumn Day

Beloved, mine
Even though I may die this day

My heart belongs to you
In our brief time as one
No other shall
Ever hold such fire

For when I gaze into your eyes
Only stars can compare
Reality is swept aside
Enchantment your gift to my
Vacant heart
Engulfed in despair, I find comfort
Remembering an Autumn kiss...

Man-O-War

Lord, lift me high
And higher still

My guts afire
Worms fill my flesh

No rest for bones made weary

Battle hardens
Hearts of silk

Making rage
The food of choice

Grant me victory this sweet day

Comme Je Lèche les Fleurs

To taste the flower
In your garden

I run my mouth
Along your stem

You shutter as I travel
Well beyond the gate

To where the blossoms burst
And the nectar flows

Fold against me
In your passion

Then fall away
From me

And sleep....

Crushing Emptiness

My time on Earth is waning
Never filled

With joy, nor laughter
Ever dismal is my life

Tears spilled

Within this timeline
A thousand fold

People in and out of my existence
Ever dismal is my life

Not one friend left to hold

Questo Cuore è il Vostro, Sempre

Come close to me, my heart
Let me see you
As no one else can
Remind me why I loved you then
Remind me why I love you still
I miss those days of old
So sweet
So simple
All made magic, when you were mine...

Dragons Slain, Princess Restored

The Best of Threkjshanelle: Collection Three

Clean

When you find my twice torn spirit
Apply the kiss that starts me healing
Send me back to innocence
Heal my ravaged heart's past tense

As if chains were lifted from me
Will this pain subside
As you lay your hands upon me
Your touch is cleansing

Make the filth and baggage
Yet another to be rid of

Peel away the layers
All of it must go away
Send me back to myself
To a time when I was clean

Crunchy Eyelids Flaming

Yummy buckets fill my fridge
Eyelids have it
Yeah, yeah

Burn a soul-kiss into my forehead
Crunchy eyelids
Yeah, yeah

Smack a tree with my eyes shut
My poor car, a tragedy

Set aflame in all but glory
Crispy optics are my friend

Six Legs Southward

Cricket singing Elvis tunes
I can't hear them
Ears are wrapped

Beetles painting torrid sunsets
I cannot see
My eyes are trapped

Walking where the desert calls you
Wish to follow
Yet I am tied here

Six legs southward
Mine are bound
As eight legs stole me from the ground

Po' Folk

Biscuit lickin' memories of meals gone by
Every dime is like treasure

Had car, now only got a hubcap
And you wonder why I feel like cryin'
Please don't get me wrong
People somewhere
You know is worst off than I is

Only, I still can't help but think
Nicer things, would be nicer
Even if it was some shoes with laces

Dirt and rags is all I know
All I had, I have no more
Yet I'm hopeful, yet I'm hopeful

Adrift

I felt a closeness to this world
To belong was all I longed for

Old I am, and bitter now
I set myself apart and how

Could it come to this
The cold and distant stare
We have hurt each other so

To forgive ten billion souls
For killing me day after day

With sneers and snipes
With pettiness of all sorts

That is how it came to this
The bold, resilient glare

I resolve to hurt no more

Bus Ride

Rollie-pollie troll-freak wobbles on
Muttering aloud, annoying at best
She is followed by a "thing"
Matted hair, greasy face (smells like last year's tragedy)

Prissy missy, next stop
Skanky old crone stares at me
Little "angels"... not,
Banter-bicker, back-n-forth

Tub-o-lard, works for fast-food
(Looks like fast-food worked for him)
Druggy thuggy picking his nose
A scary sight to be sure

Miles roll by, on and off they go
Time for me, a standstill
Stick figure driver
Meets and greets and says good-byes
Cannot wait for home and something less "normal"

Death Row

Hanging by a thread
Waiting to die
Waiting to matter,
To no one

Truth

In your eyes I search for it
In your lies I find empty promise

Nowhere is a place
Where my heart lives
Where hope never comes to visit

You speak to me
With half yourself

The other is in shadows
Hiding pieces of a tragedy

Only you could find
So tragic…

Recipe

2 cups of tenderness

10 ½ tablespoons of talking and listening (discard any lies)

4 teaspoons of loving glances

7 cups of steaming passion

12 ½ dozen I love you's (sprinkle liberally)

1 pinch Romantic Spice

20 kisses

Mix ingredients well with patience and well-kept promises. Let stand for exactly one lifetime. DO NOT LET COOL. Keep heated with steaming passion and loving glances when necessary. Add Romantic Spice daily. Enjoy kisses poured over sweet tender moments.

Live happily ever after…

Gone Missing

Where is she now
My princess, my angel

Where is she now
There's a hole in my heart

I pray may God keep her
So safe and so strong

And bring her back home quickly
And heal this love-wound

Andy Cooper © 2010

She Plays with Fur, Mutated

The Best of Threkjshanelle: Collection Four

Sins of the Father

I am cursed
I pay for my father's indiscretions
Felling like Jesus
Baring Weight

Yet, I shan't be glorified

She Who Loves Me

In my fear I love you so
Can't dare
Reveal my truth to you

Every time you look my way

I feel the fire in your eyes
Burning hope into this life
Of dismal dark, and ever-rain

Schiavo

A murder that was subtle
A killing planned by one
Yet shared by many

Will he suffer
Will he ache
As she did
Searching through an empty stomach

Finding nothing more
Than politics and betrayal

Will he suffer
Will he ache
As I did, that long and lonely day

Porkbelly Reverse Engineering

Big and sloppy did you say?

We can melt those pounds away

Try us now!

For 30 days

Fast results!

You'll be amazed

08/25/04

When I found a way to get you back

Everything would have to wait

Finding you was all that mattered

One heart repaired, one life un-shattered

Ugly deeds once thought unpunished

Got a taste of our true justice

Here and now we stand

To show the strength of the RellianStorm
Be gone
And never tread on Colorado soil again
Keep well back or keep well dead…

Vermillion Blue

My blood runs sad
Vermillion Blue colors my existence
Spanish hallways echo
Those days I walked with you
And now, must walk alone
Lace and shadows
Retell a love that no one
Could ever take from me
Or break me of
Yet here I stand, alone, so alone

Disease

Burning through me as a fire
Pain is your mapmaker
Agony your friend

Can you have no pity
Will you *not* attack me

Destroyer
Life stealer
King of sorrow

How intimate you are
Caressing every fiber
Suckling every soul light
Till I am a husk
Rotting in a retched grave

Sexy Tan

Basking in the glow of you
Lacquered in hues of ebony
And exotic spice

Can I resist someone so fine,
Keeping me on edge?

I find that I have lost myself
In the shadows
Of your enticing darkness

Chiavare

To find you deep within me
Almost blending
Like one skin

This is how I feel inside us
This is how I feel beyond me

A dream without sleeping

This is how I feel beyond us
This is how I feel inside me

Symphony in Ghetto Major

Who is you
You broke my cat
Why you wanna

Be like that

Stole my shoes
And swiped my hat
Why you wanna
Be like that

Is you suave
Is you cool
I think not
You's a fool

Rock On

The Best of Threkjshanelle: Collection Five

Jesus Contact Lenses

 If I could wear Him on my eyes
What would I see

How should I feel

Deity sight might drive me mad

Would I finally understand it

The why's of war

The when's of waiting for an answer

Will my spirit cling to pain and old wounds
 Or is love to be my 20-20

Jody Watley

Take me back to yesterday
When I was young
So full of hope
Immersed in love

Your words were pure
And laced with truth
Melodies so simple
And intricate

Forsaken you
For far too long
When hearts burned cold
Then faded

A brand new day
Erased the gray
From memories
Bleak and tainted

Affairs of the heart
Made me turn away
A stolen moment
Brought me home

Depression

I fall into myself
I lock the door behind me

No one gets inside my heart
No one gets inside my head

Misery is my bride
Till life do us part…

Trippin'

Sci-fi biscuit
I was feelin' fine
Buzzin' off a 40
As I drove away

Skin turn to green
Like Frankenstein

Fuzz at my back
Wanna ruin my day

Step on the gas
Doin' 99
Catch me if you can
As I fly away

Kissed by a tree
Just broke my spine
Pass from this world
That's the price you pay

Slab

Here I find you
Rest in peace

Once so lively
Now deceased

Will you rise up from the dead
With wounds healed upon your head

Where the bullets struck you hard
Life hath dealt, the loser's card

Of Destiny & Treasure

Stand together my kinsrelg
Ours is a strong threkjshanelle

Of noble and caring souls

The future is a path
We travel together

We have a wealth
Few others mind to acquire

Love for one another

Kiona the Bridge

Between cultures
Between ethnic boundaries

And warring houses

You are the bridge

You are the peace

That draws us together

You are the love

That binds us whenever

Dark times befall we

Ottmar Liebert

Simple elegance
For a complex world

I welcome the melody
At the end of the day
As I surrender 2 love

Waiting 4 stars 2 fall

Condemned

You would think that
To live in honor and grace
Would be revered

Yet here I lay in a pool
Of your contempt
With you wanting more from me

You drink me dry
Leaving my very existence
An empty husk to shrink
And blow away

Secondhand Existence

The thrift store is my shopping mall
My brother gave me a three-wheeled Chevy
I'm stylin' now

My lunch is in a paper sack
I've used a dozen times before

I spy my wee one on the floor
Playing with a hand-me-down

I swear one day things will change
I swear one day I'll have "new"

Until it falls into my lap
I make the best
Of this secondhand existence

Little Eyes, Big World

The Best of Threkjshanelle: Collection Six

Annie Liebowitz

When first I encountered it
Only awe could describe

Wonders upon wonders
You made the lens a treasure box

Over whelming images
Unleashed

Reality and the bizarre
Often are one in the same

Certainly you will not stop
Keeping us ever bedazzled

Wrong Side of the Bed

Is it all a joke
My misspent, malfunctioned life
Finding
Only
Regurgitated
Turmoil
Year after year
Not a friend left to care
Old and worn down
Wondering why I bother to breathe

Realmlord's Holding Ground

No, I say
Not this time
Not this spirit
You shall not break me

You cannot shake me

I am of the Storm

A Rellian through and through

I may stumble

My face may hit the ground

But once I rise
And I will rise
You shall wish
There were some place

To hide you....

Frida

Why am I in love with you
Long gone from here, tis' true
I never really met you
Never held you in my arms
Yet here I am
Feeding on a lover's kiss
Only given to me in my dreams

My God, I'm Normal!

Losing my grip on fantasy
Spiraling into control
Help me
I'm so un-helpless
Help me
I'm so responsible
Cannot stand to find myself
Take me back
To where I don't belong....

Beat Me Till I Like It

Yeah little hottie
I be bad
Naughty and rotten to the core

Spank me darlin'
Spank me
Smack me as I smile for more

Bruise me
Use me
Lose me in a sea of pain

Bash me
Thrash me
Smash me until I'm whole again

Drunken Sorrow

In love with a yesterday
A memory so sweet
Were I to have that day back
Would I be a better man

Would I be the man of my dreams
Or still a stupid sod
A nothing in the mirror that I stare at

She made me someone
She was the spice of it

I lost her
On a cold and windy February day
Sorrow is me, ever-always
Sorrow is me

Shotgun Shoeshine

I'll polish your patent leather
Just like I polish my 12-gauge

You look down upon my profession, and myself

Reminds me of lookin'
Down the barrel
At a target in my sights

Either way, I'll polish you off

Walking into Wasted Spaces

In and out of their lives
These do-nothing beings
These wasteland wanderers

Hoping to make a difference
Fooling myself along the way
Never shall they be

Anything more, than emptiness & shadows....

This Fire

Don't let it die
The dream, the heart-set
The ever-thirsting desire

Lesser minds
Will try to crush it
The faint of heart
Attempt to hush it

Don't let the flames of destiny
Fade into empty regret

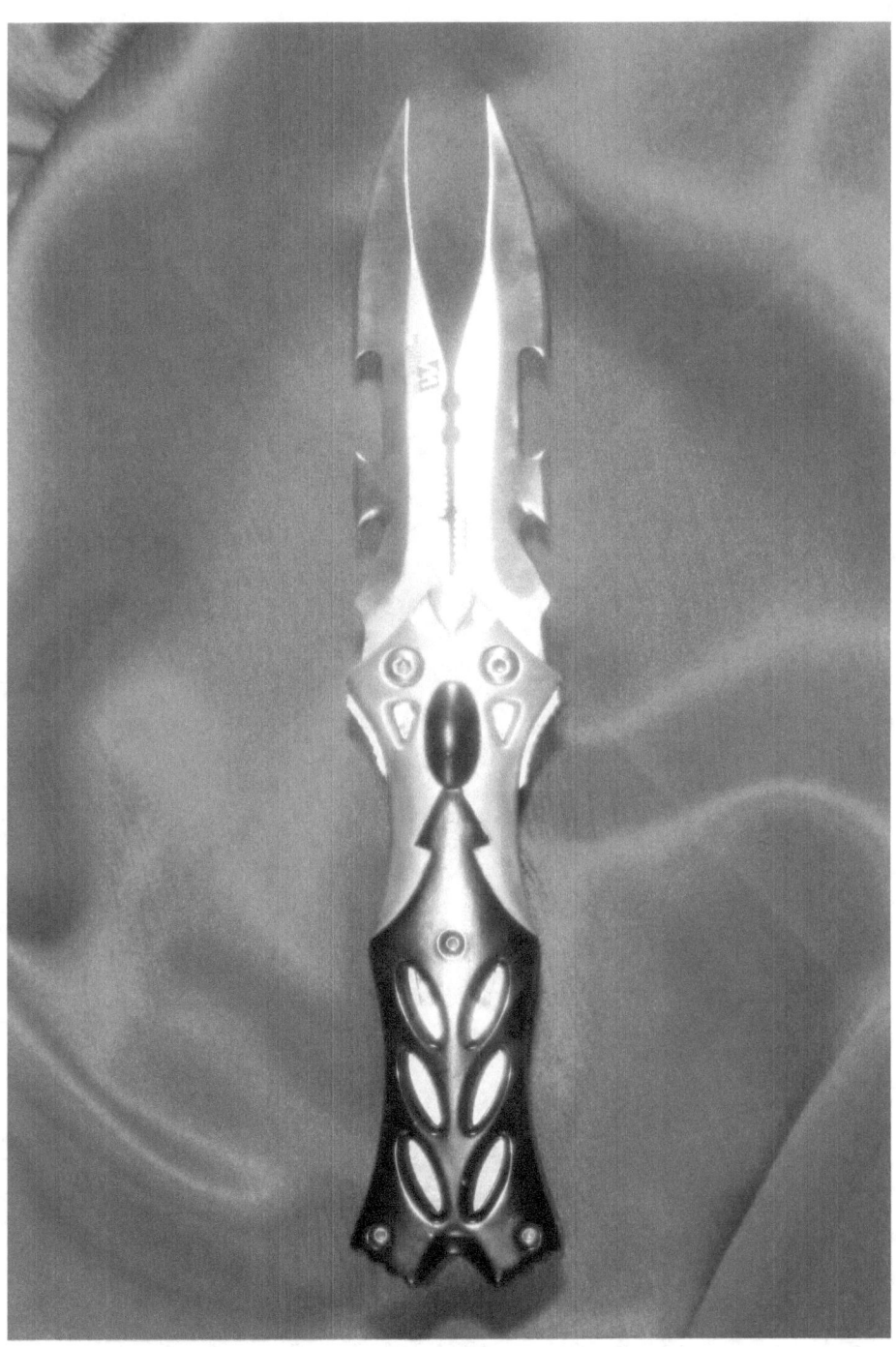

The Storm, it Does Rain Daggers

The Best of Threkjshanelle: Collection Seven

Nuclear Winter

White with despair
Is my blackened heart

A traitor to me
I've become in part

An anger that snows
Burns ice through my veins

Do you miss me

A shadow that whispers
It whispers my name

It swallows me up
And snuffs out my flame

An anger that snows
Burns ice through

Do you wish me? Dead...

Open Wound

My love for you
An open wound

Will you mend it
Make it better

Or salt it
And bring me madness

The End

Didn't think it could come to this
Couldn't know it would hurt so bad

No longer touch, no longer kiss
No longer anything of what we had

Holding on like leaves in an autumn wind
Then comes the fall, we spiral down

As I felt the clouds set in
I knew that I would surely drown

In a pool of your contempt

Paramour de Taos

She calls to me
My Navajo princess
Hair of blackened silk
And eyes, so dark with mystery

No other can replace her
In my heart, or in my thoughts

As turquoise skies fade to onyx hues
Our shadows bleed together

As fires of the night

Cat Dancing

I try to fool myself
Into thinking I'm alright
Knowing that I'm only
Cat-dancing my way
Through a life of pain

As clever as I think I am
No truth could be truer
I rot inside
I yearn for inner peace

A time machine would serve me well
To set right, the moment
That sent me on a crooked path
Wandering down a misery without end

Lust

It will drive me
It will take me over

This taste for longing
This unfed tapeworm

Is it you who weakens me so

Dream with Me

Unhappily ever-after
We live it
We regret it

What could have been
What should have been

Would it hurt to imagine
That, which may have
That, which bleeds into our thoughts

We realize too late
That we were made to be

Broken Halo

Waking with angels in hell
No other path to take
Shall I ever stand once more
In pure & loving light

Sinners dust hath seeped into my fiber
My skin, a cloth I cannot wash
So tainted with the sorrows
Of those I've come to aid & raise

Is it my fate to bleed
As they do

To lament in perpetual despair
Wishing my eternal life would end

War is Only Skin Deep

A Jekyll and Hyde syndrome
I war with me, when I'm alone

This side of myself
Feels no shame
Tis' the other
Who takes the blame

For wretched deeds
For fallen promises
This Fredrick march, is a path I follow

Heart Nouveau

She came into my life
As life came out of me

Both caged by circumstance
Yearning to be free

Never knowing that I was my own answer
Yet she was the key

A thousand lifetimes shared
In one glance
One passing
One shared memory

Winds of Change

The Best of Threkjshanelle: Collection Eight

Pensive

Twilight years I reflect
On all I've done, and haven't yet

Love and hatred have twisted their meanings
I don't see things as once I did
As when youth coursed through me
As when what others thought meant more

Than it ever could now

Blame

When you cannot face yourself
When your ego needs a stroke
You come to me

I am pushed into the spotlight
Awaiting the stones
Awaiting the curses and sneers

I am the whipping post
I am the wasted meat
Point a finger
And there I stand

Day After

In your arms,
I am safe from myself....

Monkey-flavored Whore

As I stagger through the door
I realize, like never before

She did me in
Gave me this grin

That little Monkey-flavored Whore

1,2,3, and 4....
Count me out
I'm on the floor

It's in a spin
This world I'm in

Feel like a bottle washed up on shore

(Insert musical interlude here)

Can't remember the night before
Why was I sleepin' here on the floor

Did not escape
That crazy ape
That little Monkey-flavored Whore

Misunderstanding

She just stared at me
When I asked her,

Softer, slower
Harder, faster

She called me pervert
Slapped my face

All I wanted
Was her taste,

In music....

Talos

Crusader, crusader
Lord of the seven realms

Winning loyalty
Through blood and steel

Through justice
Cast upon the unrighteous and unworthy

Wiping tears from children
Thrown into bondage and heaped in despair

Let no one take your crown
Or your head
As you ride into battle

Disembowel and dismember
All who oppose you...

Mishap Hero

You dashing young warrior
With your gauntlet of rubber
Hold me in your arm (the good one)

Regale me with stories
Of battles with monsters
Such as two-headed chickens
And roaches of fire

I swoon at the sight
Of your one-toothed smile

I am taken to faraway days
As I gaze into your dreamy glass eye

Blood on Lace

Sun is shining
But not on me
Perpetual darkness is my lover

Life's a curse
All so hollow
Kiss me quick before I shadow

Wasted Nosferatu State

My open smile
Your open throat
I taste your spirit

Drunken maiden
Fall alone
With no one round to hear it

Aftertaste
Is after me,
And now, I start to stumble

Can't refrain a bloody word
All I do is mumble

Revenge on me
Though not lasting
Make me pay for
Thoughtless tasting

Mosh Pit Medical

Cure me from sanity
Heal me from reality
Crank up the medicine
Louder than loud

Bash it up and smash it all
Answer when you hear the call
Hurling other fellow creatures
Into the crowd

Of Onyx & Skystone

The Best of Threkjshanelle: Collection Nine

Remains of the Day

They lay gutted and strewn
Along the battled soaked landscape
Those you hated, those you loved
Some never saw it coming
Others could smell it on the wind

The carnage....
The acid as fire....
Soaking anguish into flesh
Sending chill to the bone

The only thing palatable
Is the sweet taste of victory

Flight

Kiss me with another's lips
Betray me without care

Was it for the thrill, my love
Or a grudge
Of which I am not aware

I tried to live up to my honor
All the while, a fool for you

No longer

Real life beckons

Good-bye

Broken Angel

Hatred burning through my veins
Make young and whole again
You may think me quite insane
But that's what makes me roll my friend

Pain....
I'm starting to come detached
From memories long dispatched
Of moral upstanding, trashed
By life as a reality
Seek me out and you shall see
The fallen soul, this is me
The fallen soul. This is me....

Love is absent from my name
I have failed forevermore
Never hoping to regain
Never hoping to restore

Pain....
Has hardened my heart, be still
Don't preach to me what you will
Your piety holds no thrill
I am lost and asleep, in this
All started with just one kiss
From a lover with sin as bliss
From a lover. Her sin was bliss....

Brain Bashed Out, Ever-lovingly

In one breath you tell me
That I'm special, the best you ever had

But then your gears are switched
I am nothing but a witch
With a "b" in "w's" stead

How did I,
Receive such honor
To be a star
Within you ire

When will I play a part
In a new production
Of your heart
The one that's overdue

Cast me in another role
Not one where you lose control
Or I'm a blight upon your soul
But that is beyond you, is it not

Wendy O

All dolled up
Lookin' raunchy and mean
Hail, all hail
The punk rocker queen

Blew me away
When she came on the scene
Hail, all hail
The punk rocker queen

Now I look back
On the days of my youth
Wail, oh wail
The God-awful truth

When I found out
That her life had gone *poof*
Wail, oh wail
The God-awful truth

Daddy, Accept Me

When little boys
Grow into little men
With little minds
And little else

A daughter's heart
Will fall away
Pushed by intolerance
Marred by a father's silence

Were you given choices
Or told to fall in line
A cookie-cutter existence
Blind, leading blind

I'm sorry that I shall not follow
In foot paths that seem so narrow

To myself I must stay true
To myself I must stay true

Kinda Jacked Up

Laying on the bathroom floor
Coughing up blood
Expelling the bad medicine of the past

How could I have come to this

Sweet memories now a bitter tea
My lover is in a bottle
She gives me comfort
Yet retched pain

I have tried to part ways
I have vowed to be free

But I am bound by fluid tentacles
I am tied to blissful misery

Common Sense Makes No Sense

Your child runs off into the street
You stand there and watch

The gas gage screams, "Feed me"
You drive on without care

Common sense makes no sense to you
In your twist of logic only one thing's true

You want what you want,
The world revolves around you

Anti-ghetto Mentally

Even when
Surrounded by dire
Circumstances
And lower mindsets
Push away the poison thoughts,
Embrace the awakening

Mixed-up Messed-up Chick

I knew you so long ago
A candle burning brightly
Always knew you'd make it
Always knew you'd bend the stars
And wear them in your hair

Now look at you
Your mind a patchwork quilt
Of tortured thoughts
Of broken promises
Made to you, by a man
Who is only a man in gender
Not in deed

He has no inner strength
Stealing yours
Year after year, tear after tear
Until a hallowed husk
Of yes sirs, no sirs
And crisscross circuits

Falls into my arms... To heal

Darkened Kisses, Bittersweet

The Best of Threkjshanelle: Collection Ten

Why, Mister Terminator Man?

The bullet split my noggin
I'm dead, and now am fallen

Oh joy, what have <u>I</u> done
To get a hole-in-one

It looks like I'm a goner
My name was Sarah Connor

Santa's Beard

Santa's beard
Was long and white

Santa danced about
With fright

As pyro Jimmy
Set alight

Santa's beard
Once long and white

The Flavor of Anger

Love at first taste
As an irritation builds into rage
I drink a full cup

Simple sin becomes
A journey into depravity
Whilst I impel my blade

From belly to skull

Kiss with a Kiss

I would taste you
To hold you in my mouth
With my thoughts carried out
In tongue and moisture laden overtures

I am empowered by the symphony of your
pleasure
As you voice your approval
As you gain momentum
As you rise and fall away

A Port in the Storm

Sailing on an ocean
Your love keeps me floating
Your love is the wind

And my heart's destiny

Betrayed by Beauty

As I lay upon the sand
Severed legs and severed hand
Still unable to comprehend
Such betrayal
You were my friend

Was just a soldier
Another pawn
A desert bed I now rest on

Didn't see it coming
Misjudgment took its toll
Surface beauty
Hid an ugly soul

Life unraveled
My end foretold
Your loyalty
Bought with gold

Ghost of Yesterday

Time is a treasure chest
And a waste bin

Of memories I cling to
Of memories long discarded

I see yesterdays in your eyes
As if we had never parted
I feel tomorrow's promises
As you put your hand in mine

Perhaps you will slip away
As once you had before
Perhaps my love can hold you
And a ghost you'd be no more

Circumstance

Tearing chunks out of my existence
Biting pieces
Like a starving dog

This is how I feel it
This is life as I know
It is future and past

When shall I be whole again
When will the air I breathe be my own

Of Sixpence & Lancashire

The Best of Threkjshanelle: Collection Eleven

Giovanni

Down a path a melancholy
Wind and leaf my only comfort
As I struggle with a sadness
With a madness
Subtle
Yet so apparent

Superman Complex

Arise to every crisis
Heed every cry
You are hero to everyone

Who will rescue your emotions
Who will reset your head and heart
When you are crushed and out of sorts

You hide the pain with artful skill
Stick out your chin, heave forth your chest
And off you go
To save the universe

But have forgotten how to save yourself

Amana

The African princess,
Too young to be queen
Too old to go unnoticed

Regal in every movement
Beauty only to be rivaled
By the land of her birth

Madness of the Murdering King

Come out of the darkness
Of your anger
Fall into the light

The light is revenge
The light is redemption
For slitting the throat

For the severed head
With eyes rolled back

Such a naughty boy you are
As you grin from ear to chin
A smirk to be prized
Until an avenger's lance

Slays it from you

Artiste'

You snotty little entrail
What makes you better that me

I create beauty same as you
Yet, I do not hold my pinkie in the air

I do not turn away admiring eyes
With a sting from an arrogant tongue

Would it kill you so
To let your toes touch the earth

Saggy, Baggy, Droopy Ta-tas

They dangle from your chest
Like spiders from a web
Bip and bop about
When jogging or climbing stairs

Took you years to grow them
Wearing nothing 'neath your shirt

Will they fall away
Or will they stay and play
Only time and gravity will tell

The Dark Card Betrayed Me

Had she smiled any further
Her face would have cracked apart
I thought she was different
I felt I could trust her

My confidence was a plaything
My love was secretly shunned
I thought she was different
I felt I could trust her

In the end
The hand she dealt
Was a full house of misery and deceit

What I Think of You

Fecal-face
Idiot
Loser of all losers
Tell me how you came to be
Here in my presence

Honk at Me Whilst Stalled

You beep, beep, beep
As if doing so
Will raise my car like Lazarus

If I could,
I would pick it up myself
Not to give you satisfaction
But to hurl it into your face
Bash the smug smirk from you
Smash common sense and courtesy

Into your sub-ape persona

Delanda

Classy flavored elegance
Poured into a sultry heartthrob

She melts me
As she takes my hand
She thrills me
As she takes my mind

To thought-scapes never before traveled

Through Diego Eyes

Blue through blue
I….
Never knew

A Look could feel so bad

Can't you see
There's more to me
Than promises I could never keep

Your tears are as daggers
But I am what I am

My one and only love,
Almost…

Crimson Sky

I met her under a bloodstained cloud
There was crying in the slightest breeze

A hatred bled through her expression
And even though she were alive
She was slain, sharing her mother's fate

Strong and fierce as anyone of us
Her heart desired tender moments
As she led me into her tent
And passion burned away harsh rain

Midnight & Moon-shadow

The Best of Threkjshanelle: Collection Twelve

The Way of It

When a younger blood flowed through me
I could cling to innocence

Black and white, the only hues
In a life without regrets

As 'todays' fell into yesterdays
Many shades of gray
Bled onto my tapestry

The light of promise
Once burning in my eyes for all to see
Has dimmed into contempt for the world

I trust no one
No circumstance

I alone, am my only truth

Gone

Drunk again I see
At least you're happy

Or is that floor tile smile
Just the way you landed

When your legs
Left the party before you did

Bliss Curve

Never knew it could be like this
Living life on the edge of perfection
And it started with a windswept kiss

Arcing into fantasy, this bliss-curve called love

Could it be that I dream out loud
Knowing I shall wake
Falling from the moment

A moment called forever....

Panama Poison

I thought you so exotic
A treasure of the heart
Could not see the fate that made you
Did not taste the death so slow
But yet so sure

Your eyes, they hid the truth
Fake embraces were the lies
They smothered me in promises
A future certain, yours
Not mine

A Tire Iron to the Skull

I wish that I could make you see it
The foolishness that is you life

So down on yourself
So down on others
A perpetual blues machine
Bitter products, none for sale

Free to all who attend
The pity party
Sponsored by Drama, Incorporated
Your one true love
Your long-time friend
Can't you see we sicken from it
Watching reruns
Of "Martyrs on Parade"

Will eyes that spurt assembly line tears
Gaze upon a brighter day?
Perhaps happiness will hit you
Like a tire iron to the head

A Castle West

A fortress temporary
I'd planned to leave someday
To build upon my life's ambitions

Others would remain in comfort
A place called home
To hang a hat
To raise a wee one

I'd planned to leave someday
But not like this
Not this way

A pawn in a lover's game
A victim of revenge out of control

Black is me
For I am ashes and bits of bone
Death packed my bags
And took me on

Black is me
But not as dark
As the rancid dog
Who lit the spark

May he too drink from the cup of circumstance

Multi-breed Revisited

Condemned for how I wear my skin
Can't you see the truth within

You live in realities
Thrown back to 1953

Poor sod
It is the way it is
My diverse heritage

James Bond Gotta Busted Hosed

Traveling at the speed of light
Escaping yet another plight
Car dies, that begins his woes
James Bond gotta busted hose

Getting' ready to make that move
On a babe that made him groove
Something lacking in his repose
James Bond gotta busted hose

Fighting villains with an eloquent style
Gleaming confidence makes him smile
Gets popped, right in the nose
James Band gotta busted hose

Warriors End

Gliding on blade's edge
Flesh is parting, blood is seeping
Into clothing
Onto soil

Life is waning
Eyes are closing
Crossing over to Valhalla

Paradise is filled with pleasure
Flowing ale
And scented maidens

Dying for your kin and country
Now enjoy the bliss of death

Once an unknown soldier
Now a legend to uphold

Loving Hatred

This is what I wish to do
For all the anguish you bestow
I'll tie you to a bed of nails
Dripping water into your eyes

Oh, did I mention I would lift & slice your eyelids off?

Once Upon a Time, Forever

The Best of Threkjshanelle: Collection Thirteen

Razorblade Kisses

Every intimacy bleeds truth
My lover tastes of sugar and silk

Nape and shoulder
Dotted with razorblade kisses

A reflection of my love eternal

Elizabeth

Through it all
Your song is interwoven
With my breathing

A voice that comforts
When I am stripped
Of who I am

Flagstones lie beyond me
As echoes in a shallow bay
Call me home

Wind

I was frightened as a child
By a hand I could not see

As I grew to know you
A friend you were to me

Now a man
I feel you at my back

Driving me to conquer another fear
10,000 warlords who seek my throne

They await my sharpened steel

The Dark Prince of Nothing

All lain wasted
Under my wrath

A tree no longer stands
A man no longer takes a breath

I am master over nothing
For death and destruction is me

Attila's Holiday

Empires made on rotting flesh
And screams symphonic

Bones crackle under hoof beats
Leagues of armor take for me

A prize drenched well with blood

Nude Pancakes

Is it wrong to admire
Without a drop of maple
Or fruity garnish

Those two round objects
That meet my eyes

Am I to be reviled
For spreading butter
Only after, one last glance

Pleasure upon my plate
Is not to be for granted

As I take my time
As I am gentle, oh so gentle

Julia

One so dark, yet full of light

She crossed my path
And found me broken

My future days held promise
Of perpetual dread & despair

Impetuous in healing wretched yesterday's
Her noble spirit lifted my own near-dead shadow

Forever grateful shall I be....

Maximilian

An eloquent gentleman
Most valiant and regal

He paints with magic
His mind is the canvas

Giving of himself
He flavors the world
With beauty and enchantment

This is the legend
This is the artist
This is my friend

Hell

It, is coming here
To waste 40 hours of my life

It is a marriage
Without understanding

It is a friend
With a knife for your back

My face reveals it
As I gray
And dreams fall away

This is hell,
My life as such
And only death shall bring me closer

To Utopia

Angel Over Me

Even as I sense my doom
I cannot help but close my eyes
And open my heart

Something…
Someone…
Smiles upon my life

Even as I go unloved by the world
I cannot help but look at You
And feel an angel over me….

The Return

Hades has brought you back to me
A filth so pungent
An evil renowned

I will hate you, to your bones
I will curse you
Till the rivers flow thick

With the blood of you, and your wretched kin....

Unbroken Truth

Love, it never drifts away....

Many thanks to my special treasures…
~My life is full because of you~

Natasha
Trevor
Katyja
Kaitlynn
Joren
Christopher
Kiona

RellanStorm 2010